T0131982

Brownie
the street cat
and
beyond

B.I PHILLIPS

Copyright © 2021 by B.I PHILLIPS. 823877

All rights reserved. No part of this book may be reproduced
or transmitted in any form or by any means, electronic or
mechanical, including photocopying, recording, or by any
information storage and retrieval system, without permission
in writing from the copyright owner.

This is a work of fiction. Names, characters, places and
incidents either are the product of the author's imagination
or are used fictitiously, and any resemblance to any actual
persons, living or dead, events, or locales is entirely
coincidental.

To order additional copies of this book, contact:
Xlibris
844-714-8691
www.Xlibris.com
Orders@Xlibris.com

ISBN: Softcover   978-1-6641-7599-0
        EBook   978-1-6641-7598-3

Print information available on the last page

Rev. date: 05/21/2021

This book belongs to:

Grateful acknowledgements to
St. Francis animal rescue
The Humane society of Tampa Bay
North dale Animal Hospital

This is Brownie the street cat.
Brownie was so happy to find a
warm place to stay for a night.

Brownie the street cat reminds
us to wear a mask

One day Brownie the street cat sits
in the bird bath reminding one to
fill it with water for the birds .

One day Brownie sits next to dads picture reminding us to call or help our dads.

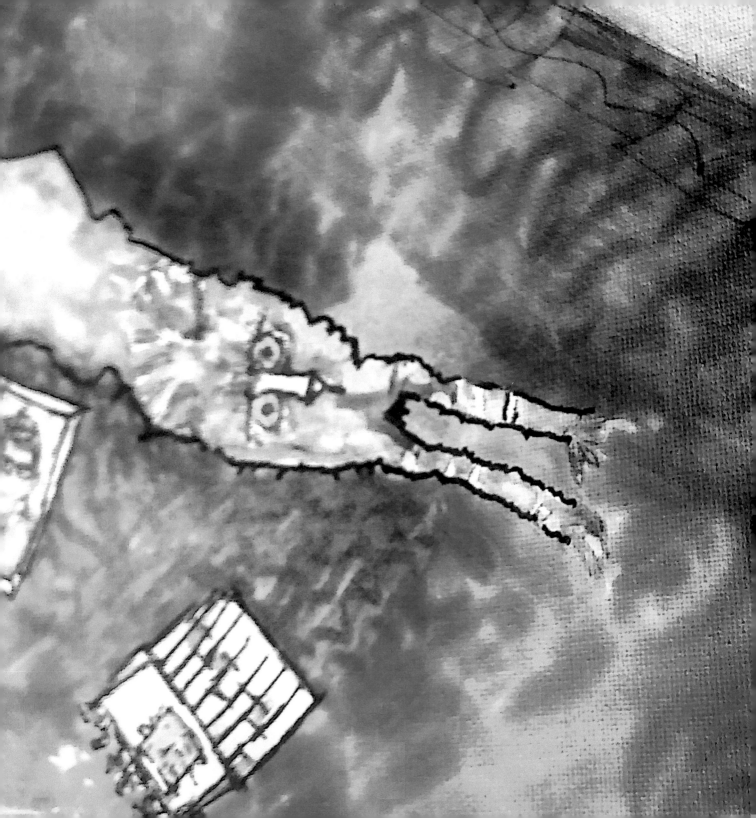

Next page Brownie the street
cat reminds me to vote .

The next week Brownie reminded
me to call or visit my dad.

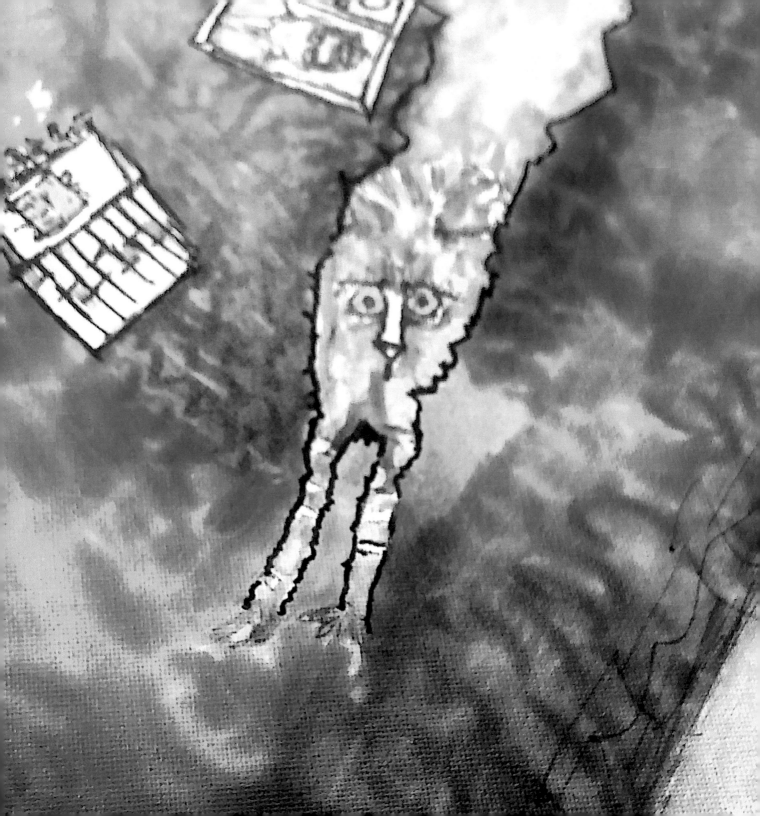

Brownie is reminding us to be ORGANIZED

This is the last page for brownie the street cat and beyond.

Printed in the United States
by Baker & Taylor Publisher Services